My Life in \

Sam Fortescue

It all began 49 years ago in a bungalow in South Wootton, King's Lynn, Norfolk. By this I mean my life.

I suppose one of my earliest recollections is my first holiday in Beadnell, Northumberland which is right by the coast. We travelled all the way from Norfolk in the car with a caravan attached. We used the A1 trunk road. I remember waking up in the caravan and staring at the rather horrible orange curtains one morning. I went fishing with my dad there. We also walked a few miles along the beach to a nice place called Football Hole.

We moved to a house in an area of King's Lynn called Gaywood. It had a reasonably big back garden and I had some quite fun times there with friends who lived locally. I went to school initially locally. I was a bit naughty and once got locked in a tennis court by the staff. I wasn't at all happy about this and managed to get through a hole in the fencing and run all the way home. I was often reduced to tears by some of the teachers who I didn't like much because they were so stern.

Living next door to us was an old man who befriended me and treated me very nicely. The man next door offered me raw turnips to eat, which I liked, and he had a massive old apple tree right in the centre of his garden. When he eventually died I was extremely sad and then became very angry that he had gone forever and took it out on his glass tomato frames which naturally shattered.

At school I really struggled doing maths because it just wasn't my strong point. But I found the country dancing we did occasionally a lot of fun and much more interesting. One day whilst playing in the playground I witnessed a boy fall onto the fence and crack his head open. I was utterly horrified and there was blood everywhere.

At home every Sunday evening there was a musical treat in the form of the Top 40 on BBC Radio One. I and my sister regularly listened to this. It was on FM in stereo which was something of a novelty for those days (late 1970s).

Our family usually made a point of watching Wimbledon every year. Mum really liked an Australian Aborigine lady player called Goolagong.

My sister often teased me. I would lie on the grass and she insisted on shaking her long hair all over my face which I wasn't happy about.

I found it relatively easy to make friends in the local area and managed to make quite a few.

There was a girl who I was mad about and I felt so excited when we played kiss chase and she actually kissed me. For the following few days I was on cloud nine!

My dad was a Pharmacist and at that time (late 70s) owned and ran a large shop on the corner of the street in the very centre of King's Lynn. I liked to go there often and the nice staff would sit chatting to me in the staff room when they were on a break. They seemed to like me and I think I might have made them laugh on occasions. They would make me a drink and offered me biscuits.

Being in Norfolk there were a fair number of beautiful beaches to go to. We as a family usually opted for Hunstanton. There was something unusual about it. Norfolk is on the east coast of England. So you would expect Hunstanton to face east. But it did the opposite – it faced west. This was great because the sun set over the sea. This made it really photogenic.

I would meet up with a friend from school and we would happily play for hours on the sand. However, being fair-skinned, I burnt easily and on one occasion I was in absolute agony for most of the night and could not sleep.

We have now moved onto the early 80s. At the very young age of just 8, I was packed off to a Norfolk boarding school. I remember being totally distraught when Mum and Dad simply left me there and drove away. I was very sad and frightened.

I began learning to play violin and piano and did relatively well, except sometimes I would become very angry if I couldn't play a piece right on the violin. Eventually for this reason I decided to give up on the violin.

Going back in time again to the late 70s, I do have quite a vivid memory of helping my nan do a load of crazy paving for her front drive. This kind of rather physical work I found quite arduous and complained often, saying I would rather be doing other things. But nonetheless, I was satisfied with what I managed to achieve.

At school, I most definitely enjoyed languages as well as music and art and certainly did a lot better at these compared to other subjects.

We did have trips in those days. Once, on a ski trip in Crans Montana, Switzerland, I was totally bullied, not to say forced, into taking a chair lift ride up the mountain. This would have been okay, except I just could not get the safety bar to go down in front of me and felt absolutely petrified all the way up because there was nothing to prevent me falling off and being seriously injured or killed on the rock outcrops some 50 feet below me. Afterwards I felt very angry at the teachers for getting me to do something so very risky.

On a French Exchange visit when I was still only 15 years old, I recall how once again I was forced to do something I felt very uncomfortable with. The family's mother, being a pushy, sporty type, insisted that I go canoeing on the Loire river. No matter how much I protested and said no to this, I was forced to do it. What happened then was that in the canoe on the river, I lost all control of it and began to be swept backwards by the powerful current and felt very frightened because I was heading towards a weir or something like it. But I believe I was lucky and somebody came to help get me out of it. Needless to say, I haven't attempted anything like that again ever since.

Something I was good at in school was singing. I was a member of the choir and partook in regular practices. Every so often we would travel to a venue to give a concert. On one occasion, after our performance we gathered for a sort of buffet style tea and I sampled chocolate eclairs for the first time in my life. Unfortunately I ate one or two too many and much later back in the dormitory I was violently sick. Ever since then I have steered well clear of chocolate eclairs.

In the school grounds (which were quite huge) was a very old dead tree trunk. It had a rather interesting shape and many of us pupils, on hot sunny summer days, would use magnifying glasses to concentrate the light of the sun into a very small dot on the wood. Of course this created a lot of heat and the wood got burnt. We would burn our names into the wood. It was rather good fun!

The school had a large chemistry lab and one night some of the chemicals must have reacted, causing quite a serious fire. Naturally we were all awoken by the sound of the fire alarms and as per usual had to descend the fire escape and gather on the lawn until the all-clear was given and it was safe to go back inside. I do remember that for weeks if not months afterwards there was a very strong, pungent smell of burnt chemicals and plastic when we had lessons in the lab.

I learnt French from an early age and later, in my teenage years, went on a number of French exchanges. The first in 1985 was when I stayed with a farming family in northern France. It was harvest time, so I helped out a bit and had my first experience of driving a tractor. One day, when feeling more daring and adventurous, I actually got into one of their cars and drove up the road outside the house a bit. The parents were not happy about this and told me not to do it again.

Something at school I was most unhappy about was being forced to join the CCF (Combined Cadet Force) which I really hated. I was and remain even now a real pacifist and I see no justification for the military – I have never liked it. However I am pleased to know that the military now plays a humanitarian role around the world, which is so much better than fighting and killing.

The school curriculum was very varied and I was able to select which subjects to study. I was keenest to do Geography, English and modern languages. I got as far as A level at these but when it came to the exams was very befuddled by the questions and didn't know how to answer them. So two of my results were very poor and I decided to retake those subjects. After retaking them the grades improved slightly. By then I was living in a flat in a tower block in Cambridge. During this time I had to consider what careers I could pursue and elected to initially do a degree course in Environmental Studies because of my thoughts and concern about the impact of humans on the world. I had a great time meeting new people and making friends but found all the work simply overwhelming and confusing. So after only one year I quit the course and started another degree course in Geography and French. Once again, I enjoyed the social aspect of it but couldn't cope with all the work and complex information and quit the course.

London was always appealing to me (something I later came to regret) and I embarked on a Journalism course at a school in

Paddington. I attended tutorials there and found myself doing a great deal of writing, by that time actually living in central London.

I was a real party animal and loved dancing all night long in massive clubs in central London. I felt a desire to meet someone special and have pleasurable times together, which I did. However, at the same time I was raped repeatedly over a few years, stalked by a white English man for months and then absolutely savagely attacked by him.

This led to me being admitted to hospital and diagnosed with psychosis. I was put on a section for 3 months and not allowed to leave the building except to buy cigarettes at the local shop. I really didn't enjoy this and yearned to break free. After 3 months I was eventually discharged.

Straightaway I returned to Dorset to be with my family. However I still felt petrified after the attack on me and hardly dared go out much. This lasted a few years. I also experienced very scary nightmares whilst sleeping about making desperate attempts to escape London but being sucked back into it. This was very traumatic. For a while I lived with Mum and Dad in their big house in a village called Walkford. After some time I was offered a flat in nearby Christchurch. I accepted this and proceeded to live a mostly independent life in the flat for some 9 years.

I then wished to be back living with Mum and Dad. So I gave up the flat and moved back in with my parents. Life was not bad. We often went for trips out to for example the New Forest or the Isle of Purbeck. Purbeck is perhaps my favourite area of Dorset and one which I know quite well. Many houses and other buildings here are constructed from locally quarried stone which is extremely tough and resilient.

Being older then, I helped Mum and Dad a lot with everyday tasks such as shopping, cooking, washing-up and driving. During this time

I seemed to be so busy that I almost put everything that had happened to me in London and Madrid out of my mind. Looking back I suppose this was a good thing, except on the other hand it is not healthy to bottle things up. However, in the past two years, for some reason, all this which happened to me has very much come back to the fore of my mind and caused me to frequently erupt in extreme rage about it, yelling my head off irrespective of where I am and who is around. This I find troubling and concerning because it has a significant impact on local people. When I am like this, my voice is quite ferocious.

After 10 years or so, my parents proclaimed to me one morning over tea that it would be a good idea for me to move out into a place of my own once again. At first I was worried about whether I would find a home but quite quickly I pursued my search with the local council and almost before I knew it, found a flat which I would be able to afford and fairly soon after found myself moving in.

Having got settled in my new home, I was struck by how nice all of my neighbours were. So I began enjoying my time in and around the area of Christchurch called Somerford. The area has a lot to recommend it, being within easy walking distance of 3 supermarkets and also having a small row of small businesses which I try to support.

Then after a year or so, the dreaded COVID 19 pandemic arrived and I noted how suddenly nearly all shops, pubs, cafes and restaurants were closed. With all the increased isolation and not socialising nearly so much, I began to dwell on what had happened to me in the past a lot.

London is now hardly ever absent from my mind. I can recall being at school in Northamptonshire and staring at adverts featuring images of buildings in central London, wishing I could be there.

It wasn't too long before I began noting the names and locations of small independent record shops throughout London. I think it was primarily the music, the diversity of it available in London which was my principal reason for going so often.

I remember studying French and Geography at Kingston University and most nights after study all I wanted to do was jump on my bike and cycle all the way into central London. Once there I would walk around for a while but then inevitably head for Tower Records in Piccadilly Circus which was quite immense. I would happily peruse its shelves stacked full of music CDs and every so often actually buy one or two.

One notable thing about London was its array of pirate radio stations, which I spent hours listening to. The music they played was frequently better than mainstream radio and there were very few adverts to annoy you.

Looking back though, I think the worst thing I did was opt to place a personal ad in LOOT the free ads paper for London. This seemed to be the first step on the way to becoming involved with London's gay scene. I ended up going to a massive house in Hampstead where being young and very naïve, I allowed myself to move in with a man many years my senior who most definitely took advantage of me and regularly forced me to have sex with him. He was so very possessive that he virtually imprisoned me there.

It took a massive effort from my mother and sister to get me out of his house. Even when I made it to Mum's car outside he was absolutely desperate to get hold of me again but I became enraged and told him to fuck off and I drove away at high speed all the way back to Norfolk where our family home was.

We were in the process of moving from Norfolk to Dorset and were living temporarily in a small flat in Southbourne. Whilst here, that terrible man in Hampstead had the cheek to phone me up one evening. I didn't even know how he had got hold of our number but I think I made it absolutely clear to him that I was not going back to see him. He had after all violated me many times. I wished to be free of him.

I did go back to London but this time I had a flat in another area of London and was mad keen on going to the biggest nightclubs in the West End. I loved to dance all night long. However, I was then stalked by a man who thought it a good idea to pulverise my head with his foot for 10 to 15 minutes whilst I screamed for mercy.

All this aggression and violence that I experienced there has led me to become now desperate for help and support. This is why I have reached out to telephone helplines and the wonderful Survivors UK who have done their best to help me overcome the trauma of London. However I still erupt in extreme rage at times which worries me because of the impact I am having on local people here in Dorset.

But I must remind myself continually that I have left London for good and will never travel to any capital city in the world ever again.

Living in Dorset is a good deal better on the whole. But with London on TV every day, mentioned in peoples' conversations and even printed on drain covers on the local pavements, it seems that I haven't actually escaped. And I often get so very angry about that.

I dream of a nicer world entirely devoid of capital cities and all their rapists and attackers.

The buses around here can be most unreliable. This morning for example, I became quite vexed when I had to wait an extra half-an-hour because the bus didn't turn when it was supposed to.

However, I made it all the way to New Milton eventually. I had a used film to drop into the photographic shop for processing. The shop's owner commiserated with me about the bus service.

I was finding my newly-grown beard and moustache quite annoying, so I took the bus back into Christchurch in order to go to a barber's shop and get it all shaved off. This was done and I felt nicer afterwards. Only now I will have to remember to shave when I need to.

Back in Somerford, I stopped as per usual at the convenience store for some essentials. Upon leaving, I spotted Adan with a friend across the road. I called his name and waved. He crossed and came to have another chat and a laugh. Being only 20, he acts a bit immaturely but he is still likeable nonetheless.

Back in my flat and with not much to do, I began once again to think about my ex-boyfriend Tiem from Taiwan. I do still miss him and would like to know whereabouts he is and what he does nowadays. Perhaps Simon (who knows him) will be good enough to enlighten me.

My quite extraordinary newly-formed strong friendship with Adan has reached new heights. The other day (it was a Sunday I recall) he had first of all the idea to gather together a selection of items from the immediate area to make a rather fine bonfire on an area of grass behind the building. This was initially okay but as time progressed things got a little out of control and I felt compelled to stand at close quarters monitoring the fire and ever ready to immediately call the fire brigade, if it had happened to spread much further. As it turned out though the fire slowly diminished and all was well once again to my immense relief.

Adan's next idea, on the same day, was to purchase some fireworks, it being only a few days since bonfire night. He seemed to know of a specialist shop near Poole selling fireworks. So I utilised the Internet on my smartphone to find out where this shop was located. I did struggle to get an idea of how to get to the shop from Parkstone station but Adan suggested we just buy train tickets and go. Having eventually reached Poole, we jumped in a taxi and made for the firework shop. The taxi driver was a nice fellow and most obliging. He waited for us whilst we entered the shop to buy the fireworks so we could return to Poole station without having to pay much more. Upon once again reaching Poole station and having saved some money by shopping for food etc. in Poundland, we returned to Poole station for the return journey. However, prior to catching the train back, Snow thought it a grand scheme to light and let off a rocket in the station forecourt which he actually did. I was meanwhile standing the other side of the station building doing my best to look inconspicuous.

A while ago, I said on the phone to my parents that, to put it simply, I had ceased to understand the world. The world is a truly immense place with many diverse people, cultures, religions and so on. And so often I am quite baffled by it all.

Money and its importance seems to play such a significant part in determining what people can or decide to do. I for one am still berating myself a lot for allowing Adan (down the road) to goad me into spending around £70 on his impulsive shopping habit. I am perhaps somewhat less angry about this that I was and have definitely learnt that in future, even if I am very fond of someone, I simply must not agree to part with such a considerable sum, lest I never get repaid.

The experience has left me with no option but to virtually beg my parents to give me money to tide me over until I get my next benefits payment, which I will now receive in just a matter of hours. I can now breathe a sigh of relief about that.

Another Christmas is fast approaching and I will most hopefully be reunited with my family in nearby Highcliffe, for a few hours on Christmas Day anyway. I very much hope I will not have another eruption of my extreme rage on this special day. I do not have much idea of what to buy for members of the family, but can only afford small inexpensive gifts.

Today began very well, everything was going just fine. It was a cold but brilliantly sunny morning and I decided to catch the 1a Yellow bus to New Milton in order to collect and pay for a set of 36 colour prints from a film I had taken in for processing a couple of weeks previously. I had a bit of a chat to Louise in the shop, mostly about Adan and his outragreous spending spree which I was goaded into paying for. Then I left the shop and headed for the nice café in New Milton where I could sit down and take a look through my prints.

When I looked at the photographs, I was a little disappointed with the lack of colour intensity but thought to myself that I can always scan them in at home and use Photoshop to adjust the vibrancy and saturation as it is called. This will hopefully improve the look of the images.

Unfortunately, this afternoon upon returning home everything suddenly worsened considerably when my immediate neighbour Robert had his new washing machine installed. Not long after he had told me about it, all hell broke loose as it started ejecting large volumes of water and consequently flooding Robert's flat. This really freaked us out and I had to go outside, sit on the bench a while and calm down a bit. I then went and told the staff members at One Stop convenience store exactly what had just happened and they seemed at a complete loss to explain why these kind of things happen in life.

A while later I visited old Frank to offload to him about all this and laughed with him, saying it is all just like a bloody Ealing comedy!

I came back home and knocked on Robert's door. He answered, allowing me to look inside and see that nearly all the floodwater was now gone and it looked far better, thank God.

Robert then came into mine for a while to chat and have another cuppa. We both agreed it had been quite a day. Naturally, I phoned Mum and Dad to update them on everything. All is now well once again.

It would seem to me that I may well have scared or frightened Adan away due to my propensity to regularly erupt with my phenomenal rage which is a direct result of the utterly terrible way in which I was treated in both London and Madrid.

This is such a great shame because I often sit alone at times in my flat just wishing I could meet the ideal person to partner up with and share fun and pleasurable times together.

However, quite obviously people are put off me because I erupt with rage in this way and I just do not know what is going to make any difference.

At least I have just had a relatively good day. I began it by establishing with my mother on the phone what Christmas presents I could buy locally, ie without having to catch any buses which would have bumped up the cost of travel.

I was pleased that I could obtain everyone's presents at the local Meteor Retail park and also by spending only a minimal sum of money, around £20 in fact.

I was also very glad when I went out to LIDL's supermarket and quickly caught sight of an absolutely ideal real Christmas tree, slightly larger than last year's one and a more appealing shape. What is more it cost me a mere £8.99. A real bargain. As soon as I got it back home, I thought about a suitable place to put it and soon proceeded to decorate it. Even the fairy lights which I wrapped around it worked quite well, however the batteries need replacing to make the lights much brighter.

Also today, whilst out Christmas shopping, I was really gratified when, carrying a bundle of presents down the stairs in TK Maxx, my shopping list fell out of my hands onto the stairs and a boy who was with his family coming up the stairs saw it fall and immediately picked it up and gave it back to me. Naturally I thanked him and went on my way.

This evening, I looked once again at a photograph which I took recently at Mudeford Quay and decided to scan it into my laptop and endeavour to improve the look of it in Adobe Photoshop. I did this and printed a copy on normal paper so I could stick it onto the wall in the hall to show my friend Frank when he comes and tell him I can now print it on 7 inch by 5 inch proper photographic paper and mount and frame it specially for him.

Yesterday I had the most desultory day – half the time was spent yelling my head off due to my extreme rage.

The technical problem with my printer is not being resolved. Yesterday I called hp support in central London, but it did not help and due to my rage, they terminated the call.

I am now resolved to phone them again as soon as they start work at 8am onwards to see if this issue can possibly be resolved. The whole idea of me getting this printer was that I could produce professional-looking 7 inch by 5 inch photographic prints on proper photographic paper and this is still one of my objectives. Hopefully I will be calmer when I call so they feel able to help me.

The following day I called hp support in London and luckily they were able to help me because I was a lot calmer and eventually to my absolute joy the issue was resolved and the printer produced a 7 inch by 5 inch print of one of my better photographs on proper photographic paper which looked absolutely stunning. I phoned hp support again to give feedback, said I was overjoyed with it now and after the call broke down in tears of joy.

I saw Monica and Claire as soon as I entered One Stop shop yesterday evening. Monica asked me whether I had seen Adan and I replied that to me it would appear that he has vanished as I have not had any communication with him for around 2 weeks or so. Personally I deem that to be a good thing. To date he has not repaid me a single penny of the money I spent on him.

My amorous feelings towards Adan have all but disappeared.

Tonight I phoned the Samaritans once again and spoke to a great man who certainly sympathised with all the exceptionally bad experiences I had in London and Madrid. It was most helpful.

If I could begin my life over again, I would definitely avoid capital cities at all costs. Ideally they would not even exist. But unfortunately we are stuck with everything the way it is.

A quite amazing thing happened earlier today. I opted to get out of the flat for a while and elected to catch the bus into Christchurch. I approached the bus stop in Hunt Road and encountered a dark-skinned lady also waiting for the bus and we got chatting. I asked her where she is from originally and she replied Panama. She asked me if I knew much about the Panama canal and I said I don't know much about it really. Apparently she lives in Cleveland Court (opposite One Stop convenience store), quite near Adan's home. The amazing thing that happened was that I purchased my return bus ticket into Christchurch but did not realise or register that I did not take the ticket when it was issued, I only realised this when I thought it was too late, after getting off the bus walking along the High Street when I looked in my wallet for the ticket (because I knew I would need it for the return journey) and could not see one. I thought 'Oh no, I will have to pay another fare to get back home'. However, most fortunately, having waited a while for the bus back home, as soon as it turned up, to my great surprise and relief, it was the very same bus driver and when he saw me waiting to board, the first thing he did was wave the ticket at me. I responded straightaway, saying to him 'Oh my God, my ticket.' He had taken the trouble to keep it specially for me! I was so pleased that I did not have to pay again that I commended him on being 'wonderful' and when I was getting off the bus by saying ' You are probably the best bus driver in the world.' I think he felt good for me saying this to him. I hope he will be driving again when I next decide to catch the bus into town.

I made sure during my time out in Christchurch that I called in for a cheery and warming pot of tea and a mince pie at the lovely Coast Coffee shop along High Street. I greeted the various members of staff who I knew there, including the charming Tom who is 18 years old (or should I say young!) and a budding writer – I believe he is writing a Western and also producing an album, so he must be talented. He told me of a self-publishers he uses – he wrote down the name of it for me to look up which was kind of him. I asked him whether he had been published yet and he said no, not yet.

Another interesting part of my visit to Christchurch centre today was when I decided to enter Druitt library (home to James Druitt of the Druitt family originally) (his brother Herbert's home was the what is now a really great little place called the Red House Museum in Quay Road, which I have visited and thoroughly enjoyed on numerous occasions). Whilst sitting down in one of their comfortable seats in the centre of the building, I noted that there was a group of older people busy playing Scrabble. It turned out to be the board games club and a member of staff approached me and asked whether I would like to watch the proceedings. I politely replied 'No thank you, I am just sitting here, thanks.' I sat a while longer there and then felt the desire to go out for a smoke come over me, so left them to it and went out into the street for my smoke.

I was near Druitt Hall and thought ' Oh it's Friday again, the Craft Market will be on which I think it was. I am still waiting for a phone call or text from Wendy who runs it telling me they have a space for me (a table for the day I can hire for only £5) so I can display and potentially even sell a few pictures of mine. (all my own photography/artwork)

I was thinking about the absolutely extortionate price of shop-bought cigarettes in this country earlier. Considering that in Brazil a pack can be purchased for the equivalent of under £1, it seems very unfair on UK smokers that they should have to pay so much, especially as many smokers are wholly reliant on benefits money which is simply insufficient when people also have to pay rent and bills for where they live. I think the Government is very greedy in wanting to impose all these taxes on cigarettes.

Having had my hair cut at the local barbers, I left the place and almost immediately it began to rain. To my delight I caught sight of a magnificent rainbow. I was wishing I could take a photograph of it, but realised that using a normal camera with standard lens, this is not possible (to capture the entire rainbow) because it is too big and too wide to fit in the picture. Maybe it could be achieved however using a wide-angle lens perhaps.

I just don't know quite what to think about what may or may not be going on between me and Adan. I don't think it's even really possible for him to get around to making his mind up. Either way, I will leave the ball well and truly in his court. He is definitely one of those sorts of people who blows hot and cold. I now have not encountered him for well over two weeks and I really don't hold out much hope of getting all the money I spent on him back. I went around to Frank's this evening and we discussed me and Adan. Frank suggested maybe he should act as a go-between.

Anyway, as chance would have it, I leapt at the opportunity to walk to Matalan for Frank in order to buy him another mug (he was very good about paying me for it upfront). Whilst perusing the mugs in Matalan, I was somewhat distracted by the sudden sight of a young man who definitely visually appealed to me. When he saw that I wished to purchase the mug for Frank, he was very attentive to me and came across as being an exceptionally nice, gentle sort.

I had a pleasant exchange with him about how I would pay and allowed him to serve me and then I thanked him and left. Perhaps I will see him again before long.

I returned to Frank's and handed him his new mug, which he seemed very satisfied with. We then sat chatting for some time over a cup of tea and a smoke or two, then I decided it was time for me to leave. I could detect that Frank was somewhat disappointed that I was leaving so soon but I think he now understands the situation between us well enough.

I told him that I will go to New Milton Photographic to collect and pay for his print as soon as I know it is ready. Then I said I will gladly mount and frame it for him and take it to show him.

The day that has just gone by has proved especially eventful. It has all happened within the confines of the area of Christchurch in Dorset (England) which I have come to call Greater Somerford. The area or housing estate to be more accurate certainly has its fair share of real characters, old and young.

This morning I elected to go out because I needed some basic grocery essentials and decided to use the most local One Stop convenience store which is only a short walk away. So after the worst of the weather had passed and a bit of sunshine had returned, I made my way out of my home and towards the local shop – I needed some more postage stamps and was wondering whether I could avail myself of some at this shop rather than having to walk a lot further to Burton village green Post Office.

When I entered the shop, the very amenable Anne was behind the counter and I immediately asked her if they sold stamps. Fortunately she said yes naturally they do and proceeded to tell me how much they were. I told her I would need first class stamps and she gave me the price for those. I then told her I would first need to wander around picking up some grocery essentials and would get the stamps as soon as I was ready.

Having purchased everything I needed, I left the shop and as it was still sunny (rather cold but nice), I opted to sit on the bench a little way beyond the shop for a while. This I did and no sooner was I rested for a few minutes and enjoying a good smoke (and coughing at the same time), a cheeky woman on her way to the shop suddenly said to me "Can't you put your hand over your mouth?". This sudden comment directed at me aroused my anger and initially I ignored her completely and she went on her way.

Then as I walked away back towards home down Dorset Road, my anger suddenly increased and I uttered some expletives which were directed at her even though she wasn't around. As soon as I got back inside my flat here, I positively erupted in extreme rage, partly at her and also at everything that has ever happened to me, mostly in London and Madrid which I have already described.

When the rage subsided once again, I remembered the fantastic picture (a 7 inch by 5 inch photograph of mine which I took and mounted and framed) which I had done especially for Frank my friend. So after a lunch of 2 boiled eggs, I ventured out once again towards Frank's place and this time when I knocked on his door, he was there and greeted me saying "You must knock harder".

He kindly invited me inside and I entered his flat which is truly replete with his belongings, mostly a load of stuff which makes it very difficult to move around apart from a narrow sort of way through which is kept permanently clear thank heavens.

He invited me to sit on his chair (one of the few which is available to sit on because the others are full of stuff) and I duly sat down and began talking to him about the woman I said was an ignorant bitch who had made the derisory comment at me and he laughed about it and sympathised with me.

From then on, we passed the afternoon together quite merrily and at times enjoyed music of a classical genre on Frank's radio, although the reception often left a lot to be desired which was rather annoying, it being a conventional FM radio. Frank is not even on the phone, never mind the Internet!

The next thing that happened that gave me a massive shock was when Frank was turning around and immediately knocked a large mug half-full of hot tea over. The mug did not shatter but the hot tea went mostly on the floor and partly all over my trouser leg, very nearly burning my skin. I reacted of course straightaway and swore at Frank saying "Look what you've done now!". He apologised and endeavoured to clean up a bit but he didn't seem to have any cloths or mops to dry the floor. He was worried about my trousers, but I said never mind about those, what about the mess on the floor? I then said, well eventually it will evaporate anyway.

A good while later, having given Frank his great picture, I left – he said he was more than happy with the picture and no doubt it would remind him of me. I felt gratified.

Then I got settled on my sofa in my flat and thought "At last, a bit of sanity is restored." It had been quite an afternoon!

Once again, yesterday evening I felt compelled to call the Samaritans, mostly to express my utter disgust and outrage at how I was treated in both London and Madrid by other people who forced themselves onto me by raping me repeatedly and one who pulverised my head with his foot in a truly brutal and savage and sustained violent attack on me.

I have not slept at all tonight. It is just one of those nights when I cannot. I have been listening to mostly melodic progressive, a form of electronic music which is joyous and uplifting. This is on You Tube which I can get on my TV.

Today is my nephew Charles's 22nd birthday. It is hard to believe he is this age already. To me, it doesn't seem that long since he was only four and I remember him and young Annette (my niece) coming to Ashdown House and them both having fun. I took a photograph of them both sitting at the table in the conservatory busy doing artwork. I am especially pleased with it because it was taken from behind them and this makes it more special.

I just received an email from Dad's cousin in Sydney, Australia complementing me on how interesting the first part of this book is. It is good to have my writing appreciated.

Yesterday evening I had Jeanne Mas radio (a French station) on and once again heard her amazing track 'En Rouge et Noir' come on and as ever it reminded me of my 2-week stay with a certain family in central south-western France all the way back in summer 1986. Oundle School organised this exchange and it involved an 18-hour coach trip. I recall the boy I knew sitting behind me and constantly tormenting me for the duration of the trip.

It's almost Christmas again and at least I have done all my present buying, but still haven't got around to wrapping the gifts. I think I did well to spend only £20 or thereabouts on all of them. I am looking forward to being with the family on Christmas Day but very much hope I will not erupt with my rage again. This would really spoil things.

Today I went around to Frank's fairly early, about 9am or so. I knocked on his door as per usual and upon entering came face to face with a number of people who I didn't know but who were busy clearing all Frank's general detritus which had built up over the years in the hallway of his flat.

I was personally very glad to see that someone was actually doing something about it because up until today there had been little if any space in the flat to make life better really. I asked Frank if he was okay and he said he was. I then went through to his living room-cum-bedroom to sit on the edge of the bed for a while. The people were still busy clearing stuff and there was some light-hearted conversation and a few laughs about this and that.

Whilst sitting on Frank's bed, I received a call from Social Services and they told me about sending me a catalogue of various things to make life a bit better in my bathroom. Also they said they would go ahead and assess me to have a shower installed, but it would be about a whole year before it was installed. I sighed a bit when I heard this, resigning myself to a rather long wait before I can enjoy a morning shower in my bathroom. They will have to arrange for me to have what they call a facilities grant which covers the cost of having the shower put in (so I don't have to fork out anything from my benefits money).

A while later when the other people who did the clearing had gone away, I suggested to Frank that we both go into Christchurch on the new 23 bus service which conveniently departs from Hunt Road (very close to Frank's flat). He agreed to come with me because I think he felt like doing that, so a while later we both went outside and went to wait for the bus to arrive. We stood in the cold wind chatting about various things, like cars and what sort we liked. Then the bus arrived on time which was a pleasant surprise.

We both boarded the bus and I paid for my return ticket which was £2.60, considerably cheaper than the Yellow Buses service from further away on the main road through Somerford. In next to no time we were both whisked into the centre of the town and promptly got off the bus in the High Street, saying our thanks to the driver naturally.

The two of us walked along, saying we would like to have a drink (and in Frank's case something to eat as well) in my favourite café called Coast Coffee in High Street. I happen to know most of the staff there and they are always so nice to me, offering very good service to boot. I opted for a regular hot chocolate which was delicious. Frank sat opposite me on the high stools by the table (which he preferred) and he was looking at a certain paper he had bought in the nearby newsagent (where I know the owner quite well). He ate a pastry of some description with his drink.

After this, we left the café and sauntered along a bit, in the direction of the Priory church (which is getting on for 1000 years old), but Frank's breathing was very laboured and he needed to stop to rest frequently. We agreed that the quayside was rather too far for him to manage, so turned back. We stopped outside the Hatch art gallery and shop for a look in and both began chatting amiably with the nice lady inside – I mentioned the fact that I have done a lot of art work and exhibited and attempted to sell it at the nearby Druitt Hall during their Friday craft fair. She seemed quite interested.

Then we both were in need of further liquid refreshment, so headed for the art deco Regent Centre along the High Street. We both wanted tea, so I duly ordered these from a very pleasant man serving and paid with the £10 note Frank had just given me. I took the teas over to where Frank was sitting and sat down and proceeded to drink mine slowly. Frank kept nodding off because he was tired.

After sitting in the Regent Centre having tea, it was getting towards the time to catch the bus back to Somerford and we slowly made our way back to the bus stop. Once again, the bus was on time.

On leaving the bus in Hunt Road, I commented to the driver that 'this is a truly excellent new service'. I asked him how long it was likely to continue and he said that it would depend on how well used it is. I thanked him and got off with Frank. We headed back towards Frank's place and went inside. Frank made tea and put the radio on. Once again it was classical music, some of which I really liked. I phoned Mum and Dad to ask how they were and they replied they were fine.

As soon as I returned home, I knew I had to access my email in order to print my new TV licence so I can be sure I have proof that I am paying for it, so can watch TV without worrying. I did this and put the print out in the kitchen with other paperwork to be filed at some stage. I then phoned Mum and Dad again and spoke for longer, taking care not to go over the hour in order not to get charged extra on my phone bill.

Then I had a nice mug of tea and a smoke or two and started to type the next bit of this book.

The day I have just endured has certainly tested me. It began with me arriving at Frank's door rather later than we had agreed the day before, due to me oversleeping (I had not got to sleep until something like 3 or 4 am.) I apologised to Frank about this and entered his flat.

I sat and we had our usual chat over tea for a while. Then we agreed it was time I should phone the surgery to request an appointment for Frank to see a doctor about his terrible condition – his very laboured breathing, severe and persistent cough and swollen legs meaning he has extreme difficulty walking and has to stop to rest frequently.

So having told the receptionist at the surgery all this, initially she said a doctor would phone back. We both waited a long time for another call on my smartphone but unfortunately it didn't come. So, after walking to and from One Stop convenience store to purchase groceries for us both with Frank's money, I tried phoning the surgery once more. This time I was told that I should call 111 and tell them about Frank's troubles which I did having had a quick smoke first. After telling them they told me I should ring 999 and ask for an ambulance. This I did almost straightaway and it was duly arranged for an ambulance to attend. We both went downstairs to stand and wait for the ambulance's arrival just inside the front entrance. We waited for what seemed an eternity but nobody came. So

Frank suggested I call 111 once again to find out what was happening. I did this, however almost straightaway my phone indicated that the battery power was very low and whilst waiting to speak to someone, the phone annoyingly went completely dead and I told Frank this. I said that I would have to return home to recharge it and this would take around 2 to 3 hours. We waited a bit longer, then Frank suggested I go home to recharge the phone which I was pleased about. So I left Frank waiting at the entrance and returned home. Once back on my sofa, I thought of using my landline phone to tell the NHS of the urgency of getting Frank seen to, which I did. They said they would see to it that an ambulance was dispatched directly, so I left home again to go and tell Frank that help would arrive. When I told him he was relieved and we once again went down to wait for the ambulance at the front door. This time, it actually arrived, us having just had a smoke outside. I immediately endeavoured to attract the attention of the staff or paramedics and told them that this was Frank. They said that they would not be taking him to hospital but would assess him in his home, so they did. I went in with them initially but after 5 to 10 minutes proclaimed that I would go out for a smoke. I stood outside the block, reflecting on all this and wondering when I should go back inside to see what was going on. So I went back in, knocked on Frank's door but nobody answered. So I simply waited there. A short while later, a middle-aged black lady, and young boy came up the stairs. I immediately told the lady that Frank was being assessed and asked if she knew him, to which she replied she did. I told her of the seriousness of his condition. I then broke down in tears in front of them both. They went on up the stairs to the second floor.

A short while later, the paramedics came out of Frank's flat. They had finished their assessment and told me he was okay. They said it was because of his lifestyle.

However, in fact it was the staff on the 111 service who had requested me to phone 999 anyway.

I then knocked on Frank's door again and he let me in for a mug of tea, smoke and a chat.

Some time later I had to be quite firm telling him that I had quite a bit to do at home and I should really get back now. He clearly felt disappointed that I was leaving but nevertheless bid me farewell. I left and walked home.

It turns out that even someone I thought was a good friend has the ability to turn very nasty. My immediate neighbour Robert came in for a tea and chat the other day. All was initially okay until we got talking about the bloody COVID19 vaccine again. Having told Robert I would most definitely not be having the booster vaccine jab, he really took Umbridge to this and quickly became enraged at me and very aggressive. He got up, approached me and threatened to do me in. This scared and frightened me enough to soon after he had left, call the Police and report this to them.

The Police will be phoning me and visiting me about this fairly soon.

Yesterday I saw quite a bit of Frank. I wanted him to come over to my place in order for me to show him both of the remaining two London drawings of mine. One is a depiction in black pen-and-ink of Golden Square, Soho drawn by me on location in August 1997 and the other a drawing of Canary Wharf and the Queen's Gallery from the Royal Observatory, Greenwich Park also in 1997. I printed both drawings for him and let him have them without charge. He said he thought they were good.

Frank got to talking about death and funerals rather too much which made me angry because I never like to think about such things. I said to him that surely human beings are born to live life, not expect death all the time. I erupted on him a bit and we changed the subject.

A while later we decided it was time to walk down the road to One Stop and left the building. No sooner were we out of the front entrance, I heard Frank shriek out. I asked him what was wrong and he said he felt very shocked because he had stumbled over the curb which he hadn't seen.

He seemed unhurt though, so we carried on along the road. When we eventually reached the entrance of the shop, I suddenly caught sight of Stuart, a wonderful black chap who works there. I had not seen him in a number of weeks and I entered and asked him where he had been all this time. He gave an explanation and we exchanged pleasantries.

Frank went around picking up what he wanted to buy and so did I. I noticed there were pork pies for sale for £1 each, so I was tempted and put one in my basket. Frank and I said goodbye to Stuart, wished them Merry Christmas and left to walk back.

We stopped for a while at both benches so Frank could rest a while. He talked about maybe seeing a doctor but we both questioned what if anything they can do for him apart from handing out tablets and wondered what use they would be.

Frank seemed to want to speak to his brother-in-law on the phone but unfortunately my smartphone had broken down altogether, so I told him he would have to plug his phone in and switch it on if he wanted to call him.

We got back to Frank's place and very soon I felt hungry and chose to unwrap and eat my pork pie. I really enjoyed it very much – it was my first one in quite some time and it really filled me up. I let Frank have a bit of my milk and said I must return home to put the milk in the fridge. Again he was rather disappointed I was leaving but I said I had to get back.

There are various sorts of bus driver in this particular local area. I have had both very good and bad experiences with them. It all comes down to personality. I recall one very bad time I had when catching a bus one day from Highcliffe (here in Dorset) back to my home here in Somerford. I was sitting waiting initially patiently for the usual bus. However, as soon as it became apparent that the bus was running late and it was in fact eventually very late, I became rather angry. When it did finally turn up and I boarded, I looked at the driver and thought to myself "Oh no, we are not going to get on."

Sure enough, as soon as I complained a bit to him about him making me wait a long time, he quickly became increasingly enraged, and so did I at the same time. It ended up with him not allowing me to board the bus which meant I had to walk, with a relatively heavy bag, the whole 2 miles all the way back home – all the way feeling intensely angry at the way in which he treated me.

Conversely, much more recently, I have had a truly great experience with another bus driver and he has in fact become something of a true friend to me. This makes life that much nicer.

I have a gut feeling still that my extreme rage (mostly brought on by my very real personal life experiences in both the capital cities of London and Madrid years and years ago) is literally driving people away from me very sadly.

This of course includes my beautiful ex-boyfriend Tiem. I remember once he even introduced me to various members of his family whilst they were visiting London. He was busy doing something rather admirable – in fact working towards the possible future elimination of lung cancer at the Ludwig Institute of Cancer Research.

I recall how once, when I was so passionately in love with him, I actually, out of pure impulse, drove all the way from the small flat in Southbourne near Bournemouth which I and my parents were living in whilst they endeavoured to find a much bigger place to live in to my boyfriend's place which was then in Crystal Palace (south London) just to spend some quality time with him. They say people do just about anything for love!

Once again I have fallen-out with Frank. I was around at his place and told him I was starving hungry. He offered me a tin of sausages and beans. I told him straightaway I would have it cold, out of the tin. He seemed taken aback by this and derogatively called me a hethen. I then became enraged with him, threw the pan of his I was holding forcefully across his kitchen and stormed out of his flat. I walked back home and felt sure I would never return to see him anymore – he had antagonised me so much.

One day recently, I was sitting on the bench near One Stop shop again and Jim came along. We greeted each other and I casually asked him whether he would join me for a drink at the pub in Burton, just a 10-minute walk away. He said he would and the two of us set off in that direction. I remarked at him that he was walking fast. As we walked, I pointed out to him the Eucalyptus tree, telling him what I knew about its origin. He sounded interested.

On reaching the pub, he confidently went in first and expressed wonder at the interior. We approached the bar. I asked him what he wanted to drink and he requested an alcoholic drink. But as soon as the staff detected that he was too young, they refused to serve him alcohol and instead he opted for a Coke. I ordered my usual pint of orange juice and lemonade and we both went through to sit down at a table.

We got chatting. He suddenly looked at the portrait painting beside him and told me it freaked him out. During our conversation, I told him about how I used to travel on the train 3 times a week to Wareham for work. A while later we left the pub. I think he had enjoyed going there. He wanted to go and see a friend of his, so we parted and I walked back home alone.

Another day, walking along Dorset Road I bumped into Jim and he was with a friend of his. His friend greeted me and asked me if I could do a drawing of a cat for him. I said I would see what I could do and returned home.

I set about searching the Internet for pictures of cats which I could do a drawing from right away. I duly drew the cat for Jim's friend and even found a frame for it. Drawing it had been challenging but enjoyable.

The next day I saw Jim again at the bench an told him I had completed the cat drawing. His friend could come to my front door to collect it some time. He said his friend would pay me £10 for it. I replied that that was very generous.

Today I was massively triggered by listening to a certain type of Trance on You Tube on my TV.

For me, it took me quickly all the way back to the massive clubs in central London where certain people I encountered pressured me into going with them back to their homes and proceeded to rape me. This happened many times over a number of years.

I was also most unfortunately stalked for several months, held at knifepoint in my flat and then taken out (whilst I was desperately trying to reach the local Police station to tell them exactly what was happening to me), ordered by the attacker onto the ground and then my head was literally pulverised by the attacker's foot for at least 10 to 15 whole minutes while I screamed for mercy. The attacker then escorted me back to my flat where I slept for around 4 days solidly. I recall waking up in that flat by a knocking on the door. It was my housing manager who had come to see if I was alright. I immediately told him precisely what had happened to me. He asked me if I wanted to go to hospital but I declined, saying I was okay.

However, some days later I became so enraged at what had happened to me that I started thumping the walls of my flat in London really hard. This prompted certain people to do what was necessary to get me admitted to hospital nearby. Once there I was put on a 3-month section, not allowed to leave the hospital except to buy cigarettes at the local shop and soon diagnosed with what they labelled Schizophrenia, although in fact they don't even know what it is.

After 3 months, I was discharged and I immediately travelled with my parents back to their home in Dorset, where I at least felt relatively safe. However, for a good few years I still felt very fearful of what might happen to me, so I hardly left the house. Also I experienced terrible nightmares which featured me desperately trying to escape London to go to Dorset but being sucked back into it, very much against my will. These lasted for a number of years and resulted in me feeling incredibly stressed, anxious and panicky, especially when I woke in the mornings.

Last night I did not sleep at all. This was mainly because I had slept very well all night the night before. This is how it seems to work with me. So during the night I spent some time watching a bit of TV. There was a fairly trashy American film on which didn't particularly engage me much. It looked to be a relatively cheap production. But it was nonetheless mildly entertaining. The rest of the time I put on my typically wonderful electronic music. Somehow this nearly always satisfies me more.

I dozed off for about an hour or so this morning which made up for those missed hours of sleep. Then later I had the idea to write a Christmas card for the staff in my favourite café in Christchurch and catch the bus into town to see that it was delivered. The staff seemed to appreciate my thinking of them which gratified me as I sipped my tea in the café.

Heading for the bus back to Somerford, I heard someone call my name and looked ahead of me, to catch sight of a certain female friend who clearly wished to speak to me. I approached her (she was sitting with a man in the bus shelter) and said hello. We began to chat. She drew my attention to the man she was with – I think it was a friend of hers. I said a few words to him. Then quite suddenly my bus arrived to whisk me back to Somerford. I bid her goodbye and told her to take care.

I am having quite a bit of success in my attempts to reduce my smoking, having the other day rediscovered my 'blu-pro' vaping device. Today I have managed with the assistance of this device to buy one fewer pack of normal cigarettes than I usually would, which is saving me £10 straightaway. Lately I have been purchasing so many packs that I have had to resort to asking my parents for donations of money, something which I really hate to do, but which is sometimes necessary nonetheless. I can only hope this vaping trend continues for me.

On looking at the Radio Times tv guide today on my smartphone, I have noted that one of my favourite recent films is showing this evening – The Guernsey Literary and Potato Peel Pie Society. It is a quality English production and I love the film overall, however I have to think carefully about which bits of the film to avoid because it features scenes in yes you guessed it, London. And this London stuff could well trigger me into extreme rage once again, which I do not want to happen. So, knowing that the London scenes are in the early stages of the film, I can only switch on to watch about 45 minutes into the film in order to avoid seeing this and getting triggered.

Once again today my thoughts have tended to focus on remembrances of my time with Adan and how fond I was of him. However I am sure that us being apart is the best solution simply because he was draining my bank account of such a considerable sum of money, which made me mad. What's more he was into various dubious substances which I want to steer clear of.

Yesterday was tempestuous for me to say the least. I do tend to get quite a number of days like this. I spent a good part of it patiently awaiting a phone call from a Dorset-based police officer who is apparently dealing with the unfortunate incident between me and my immediate neighbour which occurred some 2 weeks ago now. I have up until then been friendly with him and often had him in my place for cups of tea or coffee and chats. However on this occasion our conversation suddenly turned to discussion of the COVID 19 vaccine, which I have declined for purely personal reasons, and things became very heated between us. This led to him getting up, approaching me and standing close by with a clenched fist near to my head. He said to me he was going to "fucking do me in". We were both enraged at each other. I felt immediately very scared and frightened he would actually carry out his threat and ordered him out of my flat straightaway. Fortunately he obeyed and left.

I then thought hard about what had just transpired and then reported the incident to the Police. I told them I had definitely been threatened by my neighbour. They then gave me an appointment for the Police to visit me. A few days later I was indeed visited by two fantastic police people who spoke to me for a while about all this, asked me what I would like them to do about it and duly went next door to have a talk with my neighbour as I had asked them to. I was most relieved.

A day or two later I encountered my neighbour again sitting on the bench near One Stop, we apologised to each other and from that point on have become friends again. Yesterday I was waiting for a call from a designated officer who I wished to tell this to, but he did not phone despite me having replied to his email saying that he had tried to contact me unsuccessfully. So I tried phoning 101 (the non-emergency Police number) and got through to someone. I specifically requested to speak to this officer but I reacted angrily when I was told he was not even working yesterday. However, I have been promised now that he should phone me anytime between 12 noon and 9pm today. So I will then have my chance to tell the officer that things have settled down once again.

Later in the day yesterday, as ever, the very vivid and powerful mental images of buildings and streets in central London once again invaded my brain where of course the most appalling things were done to me over a number of years and this naturally triggered my phenomenal rage yet again and my yelling recommenced. When it subsided after a time I as per usual needed to offload to a telephone helpline and chose the Samaritans. After this I felt better for a while. However, later, during a Skype call to my parents, I became enraged once again, told them to fuck off now and terminated the call. A while later, I broke down crying and became quite disconsolate when I thought of how much I love Mum, everything she has been and is going through with her advanced rheumatoid arthritis and how now she very sadly is unable to walk long distances outside like she always used to.

I was so distraught and distressed that I felt compelled to call the Samaritans again and engaged in a long conversation with a very good volunteer about my mum as well as all the London and Madrid happenings which are the source of my extreme rage. After this, I phoned my parents to bid them goodnight and tell them that I was off out to Sainsburys to recycle some carrier bags and buy more cigarettes with the supply of cash kindly given to me by them the previous day.

Another day has passed and that Police officer didn't contact me at all. I don't mind much because things between me and my neighbour are a lot calmer again.

One really very annoying thing that happened yesterday was the breakdown of my smartphone. I am sure it was the charging socket that had become faulty. So I thought there was nothing for it but to walk all the way to Currys to buy a new phone. I did this and entered the shop. I vaguely recognized the chap working there by all the phones and we greeted each other. I told him about the problem with my smartphone and he agreed with me that it was best to buy a new one. I said to him I am on a very limited budget so could not afford a lot. It didn't take long for him to find me a really cheap mobile, not a smartphone but a simple and basic one. It was priced at just £17.99. So this is the one I opted for and carried it back home in a bag, taking care to keep the receipt safe.

A while after I returned home, my neighbour came in for a coffee and he began helping me with setting up my new mobile. He helped me retrieve the old SIM from my broken smartphone to put in the new mobile. We tried this in the new phone, but the SIM was far too small. I told my neighbour that I would have to go down the road to the shop for a new SIM – a larger one that would fit. So off I went to the shop. I only had to pay 49p for another SIM – I made sure it was Vodafone.

As soon as I got back with the new SIM I tried it in the new mobile and it fitted perfectly, which was great. I put the battery in and the cover on. The phone needed charging so I did that. Later I attempted to do a top-up for the mobile. However as soon as I tried to make the payment to add £10 credit, I was told that the bank had not authorised it. This I found aggravating, but decided to use phone banking to speak to an adviser to ask about this. Some while later, I was told by the bank adviser that my debit card needed unblocking. I later realised this was because I had previously entered the card number incorrectly. So the adviser unblocked it for me and then I topped the phone up with credit successfully. I have just used the new mobile to send my first text to my sister, telling her of my new mobile number.

Being a bit of an artist myself, I have decided to join the Art and Drawing group on Facebook. Having joined it, I perused all the members' works of art, commenting on some of them as I scrolled through. I thought the standard of work was very high, with many members showing a great deal of real talent – some drawings were quite amazing. I then watched some TV for a good while.

The Taiwanese chap who loved me, and quite possibly still does, years ago will simply never ever talk to me or see me again in all probability, very sad though it is. He still occupies my thoughts regularly, naturally enough. Me and him enjoyed indisputably the closest, warmest, loving and passionate 2-year gay relationship which can possibly happen between two people.

The very last thing he said to me on the last phone call I received from him was "I love you". This was a whole 17 or so years ago. And I think he really meant it as well.

The very very nice girl speaking to me on the very useful Campaign Against Living Miserably helpline earlier tonight said this is a great shame. She is absolutely dead right.

I did tell her that I know Kevin's telephone number in London and seem to get on well with him usually. However he just will not allow me to speak to my ex-boyfriend whatever I do or how pleasant I am.

It is at this point however that things become more complex. Yesterday I suddenly had the idea to catch the bus into Christchurch centre, which I did.

Upon entering a certain café in High Street – the only one which was open on that day, it being Boxing Day – I almost immediately caught sight of a really attractive female aged around 30 (this was my best estimate) who served me a restorative pot of tea and introduced herself as Gertrude and proclaimed that it was nice to meet me. I said the same to her. I would not say it was true love at first sight, but I most certainly am very eager to revisit this café in future now I know she works there. She seemed to be of a nice nature and may well be no doubt pleased to see me again when I do return.

Later yesterday, having spoken to Mum and Dad on the phone a few times, we established an Internet-based Skype call which I naturally do with my laptop computer. This didn't last a long time, because for one, I could not see my dear mother (she was preparing herself for bed in her bedroom) and rapidly became most enraged (as is so typical) at my father who was asking me whether I had seen a certain book about the sea eroding the land.

I hastily said that I had not looked at this book and began yelling at my father and very soon we both terminated the Skype call. I also hung up the phone. I did not even get the chance to say goodnight to poor Mum. I have just remembered that today is their wedding anniversary. I did leave a greetings card for them whilst visiting for Christmas Day at least.

I continued with my absolute outburst of extreme rage for at least another hour before feeling compelled to call a helpline and I chose the Campaign Against Living Miserably. After making this call, I felt slightly better once again.
1995 was such a very wonderful summer mostly, my God it was. And a lot of it took place right here in Dorset, England.

Me and my family were in the process of moving house from a fantastic very large bungalow in the small village of Ringstead, 3 miles inland from the seaside town of Hunstanton (sunny Hunny as some people liked to call it), all the way down to Dorset. Whilst Mum and Dad were looking around for a suitable home, they rented a very small flat on the clifftop in Southbourne (a suburb on the eastern side of Bournemouth).

I stayed in this flat with them a lot of the time. At that time I was in the throes of training in Journalism and Newswriting at the London School of Journalism which was based in an attractive mews house in Paddington, central London. This is where I went (either walking to it across Hyde Park or taking the tube) often for tutorials whilst residing in various places in London.

I was basically shuttling in-between London and Dorset. Besides working hard at completing the lesson work as part of the course, I liked having fun of course, so I went out clubbing in the West End a lot and frequented gay bars in Soho, due to my distinctly ambiguous sexuality which remains the same now.

However, this was when I found myself getting raped a lot by people I hardly knew. The stalking which lasted for months on end and savage attack on me happened a few years later.

During the summer of 1995 though in Dorset, I sometimes quite spontaneously got on my pushbike on a nice sunny day with my camera and headed off along the prom by the beach and cycled all the way to the Isle of Purbeck, which I absolutely love. I even listened to a small independent radio station called Purbeck FM, which played a lot of various sorts of music and I recall one enterprise advertising with it and that was Purbeck Woodcrafts, which I once visited (I have myself done quite a bit of woodcarving locally here in the past in Lymington in Hampshire and Stanpit which is part of Christchurch).

I do recall how once during the long an hot summer of 1995 I was brave enough to take all my clothes off in front of everyone on the nudist beach at Studland which is on the Isle of Purbeck in Dorset. This I found extremely liberating and good fun. However, I chose not to stay there undressed too long because I have fair skin and it wouldn't have taken long for me to start getting burnt.

For much of that summer I was madly and truly in love with this wonderful Taiwanese guy two years younger than me and had him on my mind for much of the time. One time I was so desperate to be with him again, I drove myself in my mum's car from Dorset all the way up to a house in Crystal Palace (south London) where he was living, although he was staying with Simon, so I felt slightly uncomfortable doing anything enjoyable with this Taiwanese guy because I felt he was overlooking us both. But I was thrilled to be in the company of the Taiwanese chap, even if only for a while. We were extremely close after all.

By writing this megabook I am getting my own back on this violent, sexually violent world.

I have been fucked around with so much for most of my conscious existence and this firstly enrages me beyond belief and compels me to tell my personal story to whoever choses to read it.

Going to London was without a doubt the biggest mistake I have ever made and I certainly won't ever make that mistake again.

I am now resident in Dorset for the rest of my life and I am so very determined that that is the way it will remain.

This morning I went out to One Stop convenience store, purchased my usual cigarettes and then suddenly thought of catching the bus into Christchurch, which is precisely what I did. And I had a really great time of it as well. Firstly, I visited my absolute favourite café which is Coast Coffee – the one I did a review of which is now still live worldwide on the Internet. In this café, I ordered a ham and cheese panini and a regular hot chocolate, both of which were just great. The service in there is always very good and all the staff are so nice. One of them, 18 year old Tom, is a writer like me who has written a western. He has just sent the manuscript off and hopes to be published. I have wished him luck several times now. He seems to be a great person.

After this, I left and strolled along High Street until I reached Saxon Square, where I felt I needed the toilet, so I did that straightaway. Afterwards, I crossed the square with its anglo-saxon cross and glanced through the windows of Caffe Nero. To my slight surprise, there was Jim, a friend of mine.

He was busy working behind the counter. I went in and immediately said a cheery hello to him. I asked him if he was okay and he replied yes he was. So I went to the fridge where all the cold drinks are store, pondered for a while about what I wanted and made up my mind to have a bottle of Coke. I took one and queued up to pay for it. Having paid, I took a seat by the window. I sat there reflecting on life once again until I had finished and then got up, wished the staff a Happy New Year, said thanks and went on my way.

I caught a bus back and chose to get off at Purewell Cross Road in order to extend the walk, which I like to do.

On the way back through Somerford, I thought about what I needed from One Stop and called in to buy some essentials, including 2 litres of milk and the inevitable pack of cigarettes.

I got home, unpacked and arranged the stuff from the shop in the kitchen and made a great mug of tea, which I so enjoyed drinking.

I phoned Mum and Dad, but became quickly enraged when Dad was trying to persuade me to cover my pictures to keep dust and dirt off them because I couldn't work out how I would do this with what I have in the flat. I hung up on him I was so angry.

Just as my rage was at its peak, I felt I must call the Samaritans. I absolutely vented volcanically to the poor volunteer about why life is like it is and went on to have a really fascinating conversation about my writing, including my megabook I am producing.

I had, before leaving for Christchurch, spoken to a nice lady at Sovereign housing about why I become so enraged and expressed my worries to her about possibly losing my excellent home over it. She listened and tried to reassure me that I probably won't lose it over this.
I recall quite clearly how when living in London (which as I have already said I now wished I had never) I used to sit on park benches for hours at a time doing nothing but writing down all my ideas on a notepad. I do not remember what these were but it was as though I could not stop writing. I

also went often to art galleries and took notes on what was being exhibited. In particular, I was intrigued by the drawings of Leonardo da Vinci, who it is said was the most diversely talented individual who ever lived. He also invented things.

Today I have really enjoyed catching the bus into Christchurch and seeing the chap in the newsagent in High Street who I know. He imparted to me a really wonderful bit of news. A few days ago I had gone into the newsagent carrying a framed photograph of mine which features a local man sitting amongst pigeons, gulls and swans at Town Quay in Christchurch. I had the idea to take it in because the newsagent chap had already told me he knows the chap in my photograph and he apparently goes into the shop often. So when I went in today and asked if he had been in to collect it, I was told that most happily he had and he was absolutely over the moon about it. This made me feel so gratified.

The newsagent chap said he would like to meet me some time. I laughed a bit in response and walked out with my cigarettes.

It is now just gone nine o'clock in the evening on New Year's Eve 2021 and I can hardly believe tomorrow will be 2022 already. The other day I was struggling to find my diary for 2022 which I bought as usual from WH Smiths in Saxon Square in Christchurch, but eventually I located it which is great.

I have decided to see in the New Year, but will certainly not want to see Big Ben on TV because this would or could really trigger me and my rage. There are alternatives anyway.
Yesterday I attempted to call a helpline called NAPAC which serves to help people who have suffered abuse of any sort in their childhood as I did. However, most annoyingly the helpline was totally dysfunctional meaning that help was simply unavailable. I swore to myself – the typical expletives – about this and found something else to do.

Today I chose to visit my parents at their home in Highcliffe. I was picked up in the car and went to sit in the living room in my usual chair.

I greeted Mum as soon as she came into the room. She sat down.

Everything was okay initially but as time progressed, I became more and more vexed about feeling threatened so much in my life. Things rapidly turned heated and I got up telling them both I was off out and left via the front door, slamming it shut with considerable force.

I marched off , walking as fast as my two legs could take me along the 2-mile route back to my home in Somerford (Christchurch). I spent well over an hour in a state of extreme rage, yelling loudly yet again for the same old reasons and felt once again compelled to call the Samaritans, whose phoneline was fortunately working fine. I spoke to a lady who handled my rage very well and having talked for some time and calmed down thanked her for being so wonderful about all this and hung up. The call lasted about the average duration of 35 to 40 minutes. I felt better for phoning as per usual.

When I did decide to phone my parents to say goodnight, I told them my day had been 'desultory' or in other words quite horrendous. Come late evening I am wide awake and not feeling remotely like sleeping. It will be a long night no doubt.
Once, during the course of my parents' house move from a very large old house in Walkford, Dorset to a smaller bungalow in Highcliffe, Dorset, I lost an intriguing book I had bought many years previously in an arts bookshop in Covent Garden (central London) called 'Creating Killer Web Sites' by David Siegel of Studio Verso in California, USA. I now ask myself, well okay I lost it, but was it really that important to me? Anyway, I could always order and buy it again.

But I am mostly so relieved to have got out of London for good for obvious reasons.

I am now down to my final one cigarette, so I am once again tempted to go out to buy more, but it is still raining out there and I don't especially relish the prospect of getting thoroughly wet (despite wearing a very waterproof excellent coat I bought recently in Christchurch) and feeling angry or miserable as a result, so I am sure I will wait until the rain has ceased. It may well mean I totally run out of smokes, but I will get used to this I am sure. Anyway I can always sit on my bed and use my vaping device which is currently charging.

Smoking for me has definitely proved to be ultra-expensive and phenomenally addictive and thus nigh-on impossible to give up, despite twice having attempted to quit, making use of NHS Smoke Stop programmes. Each time I have tried these they have utterly failed to stop me smoking.

Personally I think the tobacco companies and all the marketing which has gone in the past has a great deal to answer for. Or maybe it's just the fact that in my early days of smoking I smoked far too many for a long time and this got me hooked so much.
I have just told a certain Samaritans helpline volunteer that he is a real credit to this nation (that being the one in which I live and was born, England or the UK as it is often called). It is quite possible that in fact talking to him may conceivably have saved my god-damned life, and I am not exaggerating.

I called this helpline this evening because for the umpteenth I was seriously triggered by a certain customer in my local convenience store talking to the staff about his visit to the capital and mentioning buildings such as Buckingham Palace. I would not mind if I had not had all the utterly hellish and nightmarish experiences which I unfortunately suffered there all those years ago.

Straight after quickly leaving the shop and feeling very rattled, I elected to sit down on the bench a little way along the road for a good 20 minutes to attempt to calm myself down. As I sat there I thought, well, look, I must consider everything I have been through and think about the fact that I have survived everything life has thrown at me and I am actually perfectly alright, except for my frequent eruptions of extreme rage caused by past severe traumas (all the rapes perpetrated on me and the savage attack).

A good thing about today was how I spent nearly 2 hours working on and eventually completing another pen-and-ink drawing, this one being a depiction of a truly quintessential, very pretty, thatch-roofed country cottage right next to the village green here in Burton (Hampshire). I walked to it just yesterday morning with my digital camera, sat on the bench near the lovely Christmas tree and took a photograph of this most prepossessing building. So I did the drawing from the photograph later at home. Having finished it, I thought how marvellous it would look when properly mounted and framed and hung on the wall. To this end, I searched Amazon's web site for the right mount and frame, found the ideal one and ordered it for around £20 including postage and packing. It should arrive here by Wednesday, in only 2 days time. I am eagerly looking forward to its arrival so I can set about mounting and framing the artwork I have just produced.

I have personally exhibited the real patience of Jove today waiting in at home especially for the delivery to me of an absolutely ideal and perfect white mount and frame for a most recent pen-and-ink drawing of mine which depicts a truly beautiful, most prepossessing rural country thatch-roofed cottage right next to the Burton village green in Hampshire. Eventually the wonderful mount and frame arrived and I felt considerable excitement whilst unpacking it.

I proceeded to mount and frame the aforesaid drawing in the usual way and it looked just great when I had finished. This personal product is one which I intend to take, along with two other pictures of my own photography and artwork, along to Waters Farm in Burton tomorrow morning when there is sufficient daylight (there are no streetlights on that road) to show Marie and ascertain what she thinks about the pictures and also whether she might possibly consider buying whichever she may desire. Of course, she may not desire any of them, so I have to ready for myself for that.

I am afraid my extreme rage did once again materialise at one point today and I did a fair amount of yelling but I was quite alone so far as I am aware.

After a great and very filling meal of two quarter-pound burgers and French fries with the inevitable tomato ketchup, and having washed-up at the kitchen sink, I elected to go out for the first time all day long to One Stop to make my essential purchases of two packets of standard cigarettes, a bar of my favourite chocolate and a celebratory bottle of alcoholic Dandelion and Burdock, which went down a treat and was utterly delicious.

I did encounter Jemima at the shop and she interestingly asked me if I was behaving myself and I answered her quickly and directly, saying "Probably yes".

I sat on the bench near One Stop for around 5 minutes or so after leaving the shop and said 'hi' to a certain male passer-by when he said hello to me. Then I walked home.

All in all it's been a moderately satisfying and productive day, albeit slightly frustrating waiting such a long time for the mount and frame to arrive, but it was well worth it and the resulting picture is very pleasing.
I am now feeling very scared and frightened that I may be violently attacked by certain people around here.

The other day these fears made me feel extremely low and even suicidal at one point, to the extent of me having to once again speak to the Samartans about everything. This helped somewhat.

The Police have told me to naturally, if it is an emergency, dial 999 and ask for them. However, if I am suddenly attacked, I don't see how I would have the chance to phone for the Police because it would happen far too quickly.

It would be a case of me being attacked once again and I don't know whether I would survive the attack. Any Police involvement would be too little too late.

Also I am growing more and more concerned at all my very necessary expenditure and the dwindling amount of money in my bank account. It happens now every single month and makes me worry and anxietise so much. I am therefore resolved to use the bank's facility to speak to an adviser when they open on the phone at 7am, assuming I am awake.

One slightly more hopeful thing is that yesterday I received a letter from the local community mental health team stating that I now have an appointment with a doctor there soon, which I am glad about because they may at last be able to provide me with some sort of proper counselling and therapy for what really happened to me years ago in both London and Madrid, which impacted me so very much and continues to make me erupt with extreme rage on a regular basis.
Overall I am feeling a good deal better today. This morning I went outside in the winter sunshine and sat on the bench opposite my flat for a while, just relaxing and having a pleasurable smoke. Whilst sitting there I caught sight of a friendly couple with a dog emerging from their house opposite.

They approached me and said hello. I asked them how life was for them and they replied that things are okay.

I went back home for a while and put the TV on for a bit. Knowing that the programmes on My 5 (the catch-up channel for Channel 5) are often very good, I went through the latest selection of programmes until I found one I liked the look of. It was Kate Humble's Coastal Britain, so I proceeded to watch it and really enjoyed it – she was mostly talking about and showing the coast in Wales. At one point she took a short boat trip out to somewhere.

After watching most of this, I elected to go outside for some fresh air and a decent walk. At first, I had in mind to walk around Somerford, but as I progressed down the road, I was tempted to go to one of my favourite local pubs which I love, namely the Bear of Burton. So I went in to the rather oldy-worldy interior of the pub and upon reaching the bar was greeted and served a pint of orange juice and lemonade by a really nice-looking guy in his mid-twenties as far as I could make out who told me his name and said that like me, he does photography – I believe he is doing a course in it somewhere (I didn't ask where). I also told him about the book I am producing. I said to him I would like him to see my pictures and gave him my contact details, because I think I can trust him.

After my drink I bid the staff farewell and left. I could have walked all the way on to Burton village green, but instead turned back and headed back into Somerford. I approached One Stop and thought I should buy 20 more cigarettes, so did this and then walked back home.

I phoned Mum and Dad, but I suddenly felt really hungry so set about cooking a meal – burgers and fries. Once I had eaten I felt alright again. I put Internet radio on for a while (Top 80 radio) and started crying when I heard Clouds Across the Moon by the Rah Band, which took me all the way back to Taverham Hall, Norfolk, my prep school and remembrances of the friends I had there.
I remain very angry at Adan. He has not repaid me a single penny of what he deprived me of, despite him promising to pay me back. Also he has directed threats at me, which have made me feel terrified, scared and frightened lest I am attacked once again. I left London for good to escape being raped and attacked, but have I really in fact totally escaped these dangers by coming to live in Dorset?

I have phoned helplines a few times to express these feelings which I have to them and even requested help from the Police. They have done what they can but they say to me that their 'hands are tied'. I just hope that each time I go out, nothing bad materialises.

Lack of money is proving to be a real concern for me right now. I am once again confining myself to Somerford because I simply cannot afford to go anywhere beyond. Also I am having to reduce my smoking significantly so as to conserve my cigarettes and not buy so many so often. I have begun using a vaping device in-between ordinary cigarettes to help me achieve this. Vaping is quite a bit more economical than ordinary cigarettes, but still costs money to a certain extent.

I am trying hard to avoid having to ask Mum and Dad for more money, because I really do hate doing this. To help with this situation, I have just applied on-line using Internet banking for an arranged overdraft of some £200 for the 13 days until I receive my next benefits payment. This will no doubt help me and it will apparently not cost too much (I can afford it).

Naturally I will endeavour to still reduce my smoking daily by waiting longer in-between smokes and using the vaping device to help me. It will be difficult but I know I can do this.

I have still been thinking about Adan and am still rather angry with him, but it is okay because I don't need him in my life anyway. If I see him in the street I simply cross to the other side or do everything I can to avoid him. I have blocked his number from calling my mobile phone, as recommended by the Police the other night. He won't be phoning me again!

Earlier I had a very long Skype session with my parents and my sister was there with her dog, Ginger. In my opinion Skype is truly excellent and makes me feel as though I am actually there with my parents in the house, so it is Virtual Reality in effect.

I have been watching a fair bit of TV today and have quite enjoyed the programmes I saw. This is refreshing. I am usually very selective about what I watch because of my post-traumatic stress, following everything I endured in London and Madrid. I am most certainly looking forward to watching the Australian Open tennis next week on Amazon Prime, having paid the £7.99 monthly charge for this facility.

Earlier whilst Skyping my parents, my thoughts returned to one of our first holidays which was spent in Littondale, Yorkshire, in a fabulous farm house and my early memories of waking up in bed, looking out of the open window towards the beautiful hillside opposite and hearing the sheep baaing and the water flowing in the small waterfall there. It was truly wonderful and something I will always remember for the rest of my life. What is more whilst there I encountered a very nice young girl who became my friend for the holiday - the daughter of the owner of the farmhouse. Much more recently we returned there in the car and met the two of them once again. We had a long chat over a nice pot of tea. It was really great.

Today has been mostly not bad, despite the depressing and dismal weather conditions which have prevailed. I have been out around Somerford a bit. I happened to have a spare £20 note in my wallet so went to One Stop to buy milk, cigarettes and another bottle of liquid for my vaping device which wasn't overly expensive. Then I walked along Hunt Road and sat on the bench opposite my flat for a while. The nice lady with the dog came out of her house and we exchanged pleasantries. I told her I would now go back home to make a good mug of tea, which I did once I had bid her farewell.

This afternoon I accessed Sky Sports on the Internet in order to watch the Luton Town versus Bournemouth football match which proved quite absorbing and entertaining. Unfortunately for Bournemouth, they lost. I support Bournemouth so it was a shame.

Whilst watching the match, I felt as though I would be getting hungry before long, so went into the kitchen to think about what I would eat. I opted to cook pasta, pour sauce onto it from a jar and opened a tin of tuna to have with it. It seemed to fill me up for some considerable time and tasted great.

As per usual I phoned Mum and Dad a few times today as well as my sister and friend in Highcliffe. Our conversations were a bit limited but necessary all the same.

Once again on the brilliant My 5 on TV I watched another episode of Kate Humble's Coastal Britain. This time she was in an area I am fond of – Northumberland. Most of the programme was most enjoyable to watch apart from a nasty bit which spoke of how a rebel was executed – how wonderful!

Later I did a Skype session with Mum and Dad which was okay. They seemed fine.

After all this, I elected to phone the Campaign Against Living Miserably and spoke with quite a bit of shouting (for which I apologised) to a nice girl about how I really don't think anyone can do anything much to help me considering everything I went through in London and Madrid. I said that I fight back by producing this megabook.

I often think about two certain people I have shared time with in this community and how I now no longer wish to be in their company but try not to let these thoughts trouble me too much.

I know that during the Skype session with my parents, vivid recollections and memories of central London suddenly pervaded my brain once again and this is what triggered my rage yet again and compelled me to call the helpline. Things are somewhat better again now.

This book is now ending. I hope you have really enjoyed reading it. This is just a snapshot of my entire life thus far. Thanks! Goodbye.

Printed in Great Britain
by Amazon